One More Thing, Dad

Susan L. Thompson

Pictures by
Dora Leder

ALBERT WHITMAN & COMPANY, CHICAGO

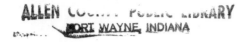
Library of Congress Cataloging in Publication Data

Thompson, Susan L
  One more thing, Dad.

  (A Self-starter book)
  SUMMARY: Introduces the numbers one through ten as
Caleb collects various items to take on an outing.
  [1. Counting] I. Leder, Dora. II. Title.
PZ7.T3723On   [E]   79-27887
ISBN 0-8075-6095-2 lib. bdg.

For Dad, Mom, Grampy, P. Kors,
Kitty, Marti . . . and, of course,
the real Caleb.

I'm going out, Dad," Caleb said.

"Oh?" said his father. He was making bread.

"Yes," Caleb said. "Can I
take an orange with me?"

His father gave him
the biggest one in the bowl.
"There you are, Caleb."

Caleb rolled the orange in his hands. "That's ONE," he counted.

"Yes, Caleb? Something else?" said his dad.

"Maybe I'd better take a peanut butter
and honey sandwich, too."

"Fine. You know how to make that, Caleb."

Caleb made a huge sandwich.
"That's TWO," he said. "Hmmm.
Some milk would be nice
with this peanut butter."

"Sure, Caleb. Help yourself."
Caleb took down the purple thermos.
He filled it to the top.

"That's THREE," he said.
"I probably should take
a celery stick, too, just in case."

His father nodded. "Just in case."
He gave Caleb a green celery stick.
"FOUR," said Caleb.

Caleb put each of his things
into a large, brown bag.

He looked into the bag and
counted everything slowly.
"ONE, TWO, THREE, FOUR! Now I'll
need my insect jar," he said.

"I saw it in your room,"
his father told him.

Caleb brought the jar into the kitchen.
He put it on the table next to
the brown bag. "That's FIVE," he said.

"Let's see . . . it would be nice
to bring along a small blanket.
What do you think, Dad?"

Caleb's father laughed as he
punched down the bread dough.
"Good idea! Why don't you
take your blue one?"

Caleb ran to get it. "SIX,"
he counted. "Hey! Maybe Obie
would like to come with me."

"Why not? Take Obie along!"

Caleb called his cat
into the kitchen. He put
a black leash on him. "SEVEN!"

"I'll wear my red coat,"
Caleb said. "That will be number
EIGHT. And do you think I could borrow
your scarf, Dad? It looks cold outside."

"It's yours!" His father gave him
a scarf as yellow as the sun.

"NINE!" said Caleb.

Caleb looked at himself in the hall mirror for a long time. "Now I have NINE things to take with me. ONE, TWO, THREE, FOUR, FIVE, SIX, SEVEN, EIGHT, NINE!"

"Have everything, Caleb?" his father called.

"Everything!" Caleb said.
He picked up the brown bag with one hand.
He took Obie's leash with the other.
His father hung the blue blanket
around Caleb's neck and tucked
the insect jar under his arm.

"Thanks, Dad!" Caleb said.

"You're welcome, Caleb. Have a
great time!"

His father waved as Caleb
and Obie headed for the door.
Then Caleb stopped. "ONE, TWO, THREE,
FOUR, FIVE, SIX, SEVEN, EIGHT, NINE—"

"Yes, Caleb?" his father asked.
He was setting the bread dough out to rise.

"There is one more thing, Dad."

"Yes?"

"Would *you* come with me?"

"Why, sure, Caleb! I'd love to come!"

"Then you would make TEN, great big TEN!
ONE, TWO, THREE, FOUR, FIVE, SIX,
SEVEN, EIGHT, NINE, TEN!"